For all the little monsters — D.C.

Words and Music by Bobby Pickett and Leonard Capizzi
© 1962 (renewed) FSMGI (IMRO), Gary S. Paxton Publications (BMI), and Capizzi Music Co. (BMI) (c/o Serling, Rooks & Ferrara, LLP)
All rights for FSMGI (IMRO) and Gary S. Paxton Publications (BMI) administered by State One Music America (BMI)
Used by permission of Alfred Music Publishing Co., Inc.

ISBN 978-0-545-49077-1

10 9 8 7 6 5 4 3 2 1   12 13 14 15 16
Printed in the U.S.A. 08
This edition first printing, September 2012

The display type was set in P22 Kane Regular.
The text was set in 16 pt. Senza Black TDI.
The art was created using pencil, watercolor, gouache, and ink.
Book design by Marijka Kostiw

Then you can **mash**.
Then you can **monster mash!**
The **monster mash.**
And do my graveyard smash.

Then you can **mash.**
You'll catch on in a flash.
Then you can **mash.**
Then you can **monster mash!**

For you, the living,
this **mash** was meant, too.
When you get to my door,
tell them Boris sent you!

Now everything's cool—
Drac's a part of the band.
And my **monster mash**
is the hit of the land.

It's now the **mash.**
It's caught on in a flash.
It's now the **mash.**
It's now the **monster mash!**

It's now the **mash.**
It's now the **monster mash!**
The **monster mash.**
And it's a graveyard smash.

He opened the lid and shook his fist and said,
"Whatever happened to my Transylvania twist?"

Out from his coffin,
Drac's voice did ring.
Seems he was troubled
by just one thing.

They played the **mash.**
They played the **monster mash.**
The **monster mash.**
It was a graveyard smash.
They played the **mash.**
It caught on in a flash.
They played the **mash.**
They played the **monster mash!**

The coffin-bangers were about to arrive with their vocal group, The Crypt-Kicker Five.

The scene was rocking.
All were digging the sounds:
Igor on chains,
backed by his baying hounds.

The zombies were having fun.
The party had just begun.
The guests included Wolf Man,
Dracula, and his son.

They did the **mash.**
They did the **monster mash!**
The **monster mash.**
It was a graveyard smash.
They did the **mash.**
It caught on in a flash.
They did the **mash.**
They did the **monster mash!**

From my laboratory in the castle east
to the master bedroom where the vampires feast,
the ghouls all came from their humble abodes
to get a jolt from my electrodes.

He did the **mash.**
He did the **monster mash!**

He did the **mash.**
It caught on in a flash.

He did the mash.
He did the monster mash!
The monster mash.
It was a graveyard smash.

For my monster from his slab began to rise,
and suddenly, to my surprise . . .

I was working in the lab late one night, when my eyes beheld an eerie sight.

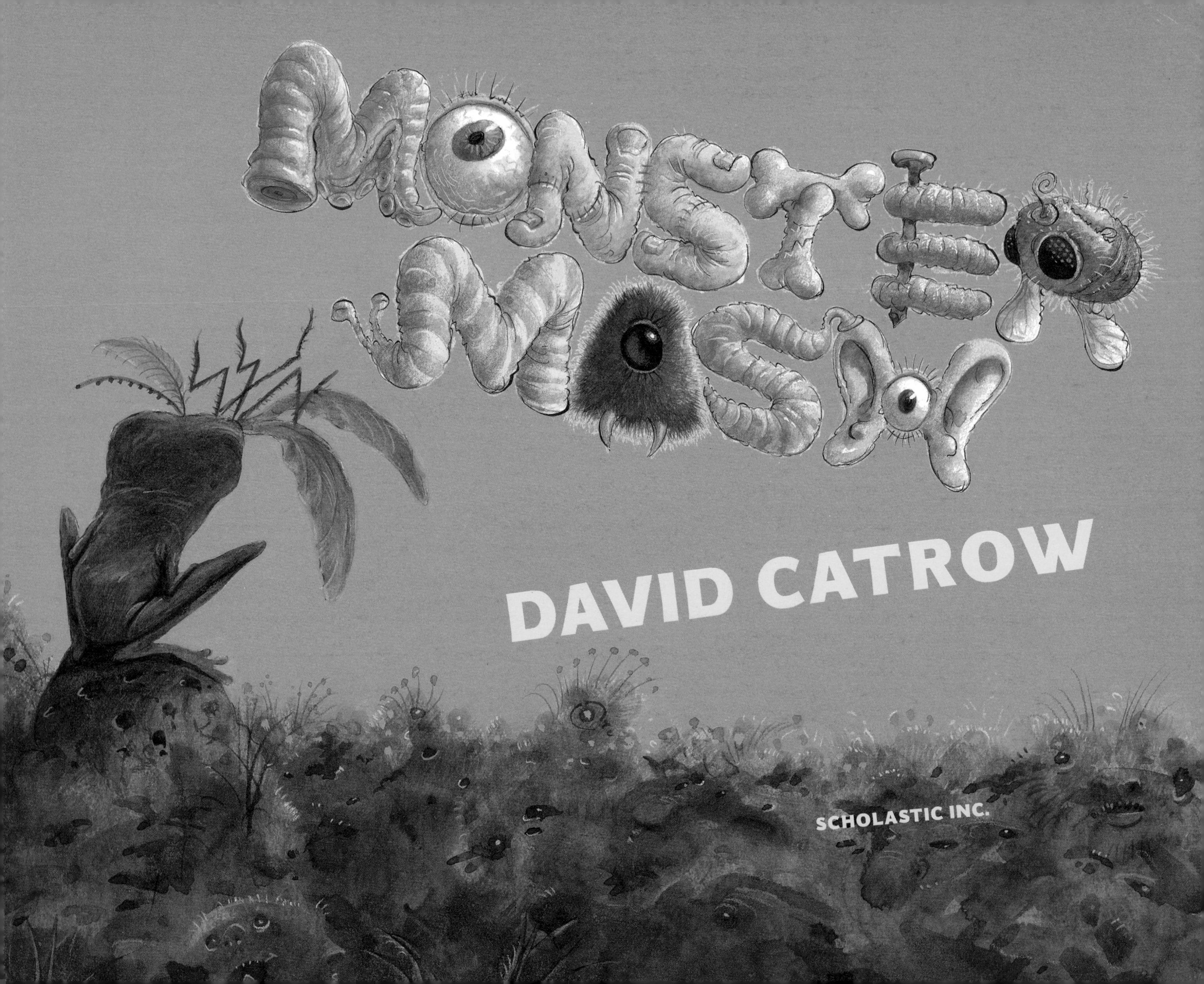

MONSTER MASH

DAVID CATROW

SCHOLASTIC INC.